Afterworld

Afterworld

Mike Johnson

Press

Published by 99% Press, 2023

an imprint of Lasavia Publishing Ltd.

Auckland, New Zealand

www.lasaviapublishing.com

ISBN: 978-1-991083-01-2

I died. That's all I know. I don't remember precisely when and where. Where I was or what I was doing. Or even who I was. My death is a veil. Behind it lies my life.

I try to approach the event, but get deflected, redirected, detoured. I appear to be moving straight towards it but somehow end up on the other side of it. This afterworld has no straight lines. Even my thoughts bend around their object the way the wind bends around a bare branch. However, a bare branch might recall spring, may sleep in its memory of leaves. But the dead don't sleep; death is eternal wakefulness.

We are drawn to the moment of our death as flies to meat, but it remains beyond our grasp. We hover with nowhere to land; we seek where there is nothing to find. Our death eludes us, as time itself eludes us. Only the odour remains.

I am indignant. I may have no future but I have a past. I couldn't be here if I didn't have a past. How come I'm dead, and without any memory of life? Is there not a cruelty in it? To be alive, to taste the living air only to have that very life snatched away. You would think your life would be very present to you in the moments after your death. You would think there'd be nothing else on your mind.

The very least I could expect is to know the manner of my passing.

First I was alone, and then there was a world. An afterworld.

My death starts with this mountain track. It is the track I am on. A track I know, although I can't say how I know it. What I do know, and do have, is this mountain. This mountain beneath my feet. It is a surety. The inky dark sky is for real. I sense I've been here before. It is the only clue I have. I start from scratch.

My abrupt arrival here convinces me that I really have died. The word *erasure* occurs to me, and has some connection with the mountain. I simply appeared on the track, no pack, no provisions, just the clothes I wore. Everything before that has been erased.

I know I'm dead because I've been walking in bare feet. The dead walk only in bare feet. Their feet walk by themselves, of their own volition. They hit the ground but hardly feel the earth. Even the sharpest stones are a distant tickle. And the clothes I am wearing, not mountain gear, not even a backpack, not even a flask of water, just a dark suit and white shirt. I might have had a flower placed on my corpse because I can smell a faint scent, as if a perfect rose has passed through a room.

I walk without effort or strain. There is no weariness, no pain, no battle with gravity, no wrestling with distances. I walk with no destination. Since I have come from nowhere there is nowhere to go.

My rational mind puts the seal of approval on my non-living status. Death is the only explanation. If I don't accept that, I might exhaust time running around trying to make myself real, a real person in the world of the living. That would be a mistake.

I am tempted to think that I might be lying in a coma somewhere, imagining this, or that I have entered a fugue state in which, while I died to the world, I remain alive. I do know things about the world, even if not about myself. I know there are lots of films and books written about dead people who don't realize they're dead because there's nobody around to tell them. Or about people who think they're dead but wake up to find themselves alive. Me, I'm in no doubt at all. This is no coma or fugue state. I am barely a wisp of human consciousness, its echo, nothing more – a distant sound of falling rocks, of swift water over stones.

I am a figment of history. The past is a dark scribble I can catch only in details. Like a child I can recite: the Battle of Waterloo was in 1815, millions died in the Great War 1914-1918, millions more have died and go on dying in wars that never end. I was shot dead at the Battle of Waterloo, I died at Passchendaele in 1917 while struggling through the mud, I died a million deaths from starvation and despair. I can't distinguish myself from those multitudinous deaths, can't pick out one and say 'that is me,' yet I can smell the sweat and fear of an old army blanket, and I still have the hunger, like an echo that doesn't fade.

I can also see things, however, invisible to the living, like the bloated monster that stalks the battlefields hungry for pain and death's agonies; the delicate latticework of human consciousness sparking colours like a supernova, throwing a net over the world. Like a frog trapped inside a piece of jade. A mountain trapped inside a sky. A child wrapped in a shroud of words. I can see to the ends of the earth and back again, which is no distance at all in the afterworld.

The world of the living is almost like Afterworld, also, but not quite. Behind the blue of the sky there is a wash of mauve, a hint of purple, a dash of violet. Daylight barely covers night; night cannot bury day. The stony path feels as soft as moss. The air prickles with the memory of ice. The rocks should be a light grey, but instead they glisten darkly as if wet. A grove of beech trees through which I pass is full of faces. The stream over which I cross is made of voices all talking at once. There is a sound that I can't identify, a scrabbling, like the echo of falling rocks. The earth drops away beneath me as it hurls around the sun.

Alive, you have a heart that beats and blood that sloshes around inside you. Close your eyes and you can hear it, making soft slushing sounds. What I remember about being alive is the sound of hot blood in my head like waves crashing on a distant shore. Now that ocean has gone, the shore receded to an impossible distance. Alive, you are a plaything of gravity; you stand tall under a heavy sky. What I remember about being alive is the way my feet would strike the earth with surety and confidence, driven by a thudding heart.

My body has gone silent. I cannot hear any faint gurgle of digestion, the sharp air in my chest, sensations and bodily pressures. I can no longer feel the prickle of my electrical system, the soft hum of my aura.

Only the mystery remains.

I have no way of measuring time. If I were here a million years, I would still have died only a few moments ago. The few moments ago keeps following me like a lost dog. I can't get ahead, pull away, get one up on time. My death is right behind me.

I track time in terms of my emotions. I was indignant, angry even, at being thrust here, but as my feet kept walking, my feelings changed. A past tense was created. There is, then there was. I like having a was, even if it's just a few moments ago. We need time for any kind of existence at all, even in Afterworld. Having a past, a momentary one, is a promising start. Was a promising start. Will be a promising start. I am pitched out of my past into a new present moment.

The change began when I realized that this territory was known to me. Not only had I been here before but I'd spent a lot of time here. At last, some knowledge! Something concrete. As solid as the mountain itself which stretched miles beneath my feet. My feet knew this place. My whole body knew it too. My body fitted. My body fitted the air as my feet fitted the ground. My consciousness fitted everything.

I began to expand with happiness as I followed familiar trails, recognise mineral smells and greeted landmarks like old friends; a bend in the track, a burst of red mistletoe, a rock riven by a jagged crack like lightning, a shy stream hidden by overhanging beech trees, a mossy bank with black mushrooms. A wooden bridge. Some patchy orange moss like an artwork. This was more like it! Everything I saw, I recognised. I was free. Everything was free. Everything a jubilation, the sky a festival of blue, the earth a cavalcade of wonders.

I could see the shapes inside things. Everything has an inner shape. There was a rock looking like a giant frog contemplating a leap to the stars. There was a dragon breathing an icy flame. A stone harbouring a snake. A fallen tree, its gnarly secrets exposed. A flock of birds suspended in flight.

I moved above the tree line, leaving the world of tall shadows behind. The world shook clear. In the distance far below me a hawk was circling. I could see no other living creature, yet beneath my feet there would be tiny insects, micro-life. Everything, even the mosses and lichens have a body, to each their own. To be alive is to be embodied.

I was happy to have a body. Something like a body, anyway. It's not just a pretend body, even if I have no blood or veins or lungs or even a face. I have an imaginal body. Like a phantom limb. I remember it, only imperfectly, uncertainly. My body has been severed from me but I can still feel it. I am receiving signals from its non-existence. I have imaginal limbs and arms, torso and chest. All those things that have been erased. And I still have a hunger, not for food, or solace, but for the next moment, and the moment after that. I hunger after time and memory. I am haunted by the missing context.

The ghosts people see could be images created by the dead remembering their bodies, being reminded of their bodies. Reminding the world of their bodies. From the imaginal realm, memory and imagination spring – and mingle. Only imperfectly. Always imperfectly. Memory in bare feet. The smudged imprint. The muddy stream. The soft blur of my feet on the mountain path. The receding cry of a falcon.

I have an imaginal mind too, which makes a crackling sound like sticks breaking or distant pistol shots bent by the wind, as if there's a war going on just around the corner of time. There is a network of fine lines on the surface of the night sky I don't remember at all. I don't believe the living can see them, but I can trace them with my fingertips, a fine latticework of shifting colours. This is not quite the known world.

A humming, faintly as if from very far off, comes from everywhere. It's not a sound that could be made by the human throat, but I know what it is. It is the echo left over from creation, the Big Bang that blew hot breath into the void. The echo of that event goes on forever in time and space. Scientists have heard it on their instruments and call it the cosmic microwave background. I'm not sure how I know that, but I do. I hear it as a thunderous organ note, slowly fading but never entirely fading. It's the sound of a universe being born. A universe that goes on being born.

As I walked along the mountain trail, I created the time in which to walk along the mountain trail. It was my feet that brought the trail into existence by connecting to it. I did not merely discern the trail ahead, but brought it into existence as concrete image. Without me there to see it, it wouldn't exist. And unless I turned around and looked back, the trail behind me would cease to exist as soon as my feet left the ground.

I was giddy with joy at this ability, like a magical power. There was a joy in it. The joy of creation. Creation by feet. The world sprang into existence by the sheer virtue of my being in it. 'How about that?' I cried, and my voice created the space for an echo to bounce back to me, 'How about that...about that?'

In Afterlife, it is not the one-eyed man, but the solipsist who is king. At least to begin with. That's the way it starts.

My feet led me to a mountain hut. I know the hut intimately. It is nestled between two large rocky outcrops which protect it from the eternal mountain winds. It's made of stone and tin and wooden framing, and was built to withstand fierce mountain winds. The conservation authorities who built it boasted that it was the highest tramping hut in the land, and was popular with trampers until access was cut off by a slip that took away a section of the trail, leaving it abandoned to the wind. Now it is no place for the living, but a perfect place for the dead.

I opened the door and went inside, pleased that I couldn't walk through walls like a wraith. The door handle connected with my hand, and that was gratifying. I could still connect with the material world. You can't call me a ghost. And yet that door handle felt slippery, as if it did not want to be touched, as if it took a moment for it to recognise the authority of my hand. The materiality of my hand.

The hut was just as I remembered it. Four bunks, a table, four chairs, a fireplace and a pile of wood. Perhaps it looked that way because I remembered it like that, but that didn't concern me. Everything is tinted by memory. This mountain and this hut are real, belonging to the land of the living, and not just a construct of memory. The world is as solid as I am hollow.

I climbed up onto one of the top bunks, lay down, and made a cat's cradle out of time and memory. I didn't have much to work with. Only a few strands. A past tense always only a few moments behind; I couldn't accumulate time. The raw elements of rock and sky. A hawk circling its shadow. The rush of running water. Orange moss intaglio. A rugged mountain hut. A beech forest, a bridge – a haunting sense of familiarity. A great slip along the trail of memory, wiping out everything behind it. The background hum of the universe. I could trick these elements in and out of mind with my fingers, but I couldn't imagine a cat that would fit in that cradle. Except maybe that famous cat that's neither alive nor dead until you check to see.

The bunk had a wood board running along its length to prevent sleepers from falling out. The roof was close above my head. I had the feeling that I was lying in my coffin. I was floating in a coffin. I connected with the bed, but didn't lie heavily on it. I sank into that lumpy old kapok mattress as if it were feather down. I wasn't tired. You need a real body to feel tired. Stagger under the pressure of gravity for a while and you will soon know what tiredness is. I am largely free of gravity and could probably fly if I wanted to. Only largely free, as I can still feel a faint tug, like the moon on the ocean, strong enough to shift these currents of thought within me.

There must be a reason I am here, I reasoned, otherwise I'd be somewhere else, doing something else. Haunting some city street or apartment. Standing on the ocean. Or I wouldn't exist at all, dispersed into the great beyond. I decided I was here to remember who I was, and how I died. This hut but a toehold, an available fragment out of which a life might emerge.

I didn't probe into why I would chase after my life. I had left it behind, why pursue it? That was not a question I asked. It seemed obvious that until I knew what went down, I wouldn't be able to do anything else; leave this hut, get off this mountain, dissolve into infinite space. Move on.

Even the dead seek certainty with regard to their lives. To know how you died is to know how you lived. To know how you lived is to know who you are, and where you came from. Your family, your tribe, your ancestors. Without these you are nothing. A cipher. Nada.

I got off the bunk and wandered around. I sat at the table and stared at the fireplace. Once I'd sat right here in front of a roaring fire while the world grew cold and inhospitable outside.

I had stared into the flames, connected with myself. That's what getting away from it all means when you are alive, connecting with yourself again. Now, I wanted to evoke that moment so that I could connect with my life. So that I could connect with the person who had sat in front of that fire. Connected with that person's life – and death.

It didn't happen. My life remained a mystery to me. My death remained out of reach. The grate stayed cold. Although I couldn't feel cold, I could feel something like it. My thoughts turned cold. The joy of creation faded. Sitting at the table, suffering the stare of a cold grate, I no longer felt lightheaded. That feeling belonged to the track, the walking of the track, the unfolding of the track, feeling the mountain stretching miles beneath my feet. Since arriving somewhere, since I had stopped moving, the mystery of my condition reasserted itself.

Alive, our death becomes a little larger with every passing hour, its mysteries ever more urgent. Yet, I discover, death solves nothing, offers no new understanding, and draws a gray veil across mind and memory. If, as I died, my whole life flashed before my eyes, it flashed and was gone.

All kinds of deaths were possible. An infinite variety. I might have been murdered, died before my time, died in a war defending my homeland or trying to occupy someone else's. I might have died in the company of others, or alone somewhere, unseen. I might have died in hunger and want in a dirty street or with a full belly on a feather bed in a palace or penthouse. I could have died with all my crimes and folly hot in my heart or died at peace with myself, my crimes laid to rest before me. I might have died suddenly, in a car crash, say, or caught a bullet, or a virus, or I might have died slowly, of some lingering disease. Perhaps I passed away peacefully in my sleep, or was dragged into death kicking and screaming, crying like a baby.

Yet through that faint crackling sound in my ears, like distant fires burning, and faded cries of grief, I begin to sense an outline. The road is littered with bodies, the path is marked with tears, with the sound of weeping. Somebody is weeping; many are weeping. It cannot be confined to the world of the living. Tears seep from one world to another. The dead don't weep for the living. The dead don't have any tears. Standing around in their graves, the living weep for themselves.

Shadows sprang out of the corners of the hut and night arrived. I knew it must be cold, as I could hear the tinkle of sleety hail on the roof. But I wasn't cold, I wasn't hot, I wasn't anything.

On impulse, I removed my clothes until I was naked and walked outside. It was a bleak night with fast clouds moving across the stars, making it look as if the stars were moving. I felt then the full force of what it meant to be dead. If I were alive the cold would eat through my flesh like acid. Nothing like that happened. I wore the cold like a cloak. I laughed into the teeth of the wind. Those fast-moving clouds, like shadows racing, assured me that earth time was still passing, the sun was still coming and going, night and day were still chasing each other furiously in their chariots. Time was alive to movement. But I was as indifferent to time as I was to the elements. Like the wind, time passed through me without any cold kiss upon my brow. That kiss had already come and gone.

My previous joy returned, and I was touched by ecstasy. I could feel it because there was nothing impeding me from feeling it. That ecstasy is always there when we are alive, but the body weighs us down with its subservience to gravity. We can be touched by ecstasy as it courses through the body, is transmitted through the body, but only at one remove. The body both conducts this ecstasy and resists it. The body creates resistance. With the body gone, ecstasy knows no bounds and can be felt in its pure, bodiless form. This is immortal bliss, and only the echo of it might be felt by transient flesh.

It didn't last. It passed through me as a wave, as the wind and the light pass through my transparency. I offer no resistance. There is nothing of me for anything to catch hold of.

It occurred to me that I probably died right here, on the mountainside. I could have been a rock-climber who slipped, or a tramper who took a wrong turn, or a scientist who got caught out in a blizzard and died of exposure. Why look further than I have to? My body might be lying around here somewhere, slowly decaying. It would harbour clues as to what happened to me, who I was and how I lived. Maybe a revealing wound or some other mark death might have left.

I found it curiously difficult to get a sense of my physical form. I assumed that I was a man, since I had been wearing the dark suit, but it wasn't that simple. When I looked down at my naked self I seemed to see a man, then that man turned into a hermaphrodite and the hermaphrodite turned into a woman. My body was fluid, shapeshifting from one form to another. Waves of sensation passed over me as my body changed. My emotions surged from a stoicism to grief. The grief came as a belated recognition that I had lost my physical body forever; this imaginal body didn't even know its own shape.

Such grief is an intensification of separateness, of separation, of severance, to the point of pain. I had to cry, cry for my lost physical body. I had to learn how to cry. Once I had known how. My body had known, had done a lot of weeping whatever sex it had been. There were paths carved out on my face for tears. I cried for the lost generations, and the generations that lost the world. These were tears of dissolution. They dissolved my body and the world. Wherever they fell. Wherever they fell, the flesh pitted. Time swept all before it while I remained standing on miles of rock in front of that rough mountain hut made of stones, tin and wood.

This body will take whatever form feeling gives it, I decided. It is no longer a physical body but a body of feeling.

Grief gave way to a reluctant acceptance. This is how it is. I no longer had a fixed sex, but a shifting gender. If I was going to continue, I would have to understand this. But at the same time, I felt a creeping despair. How could I ever know anything for certain about my life and death if I couldn't even tell what sex I was, if I was a father or mother. Or maybe a genuine hermaphrodite.

A short way from the hut, there was a vantage point which looked west. From there, I could feel the land and the distant ocean, but I couldn't see them until the moon broke free from the scudding clouds and I saw the dark shape of the mountain and a faintly lighter strip of land. I thought I saw lights, like stars, against the backdrop of the land, but we were surely too high for me to make out any human habitation.

I remained there as night worked its way through its changes and dawn came flying in from behind me, chasing shadows in behind the rocks. Slowly the world came into being, lifted into being on the back of the morning light.

I could see down to the hut below, to the jumble of rocks, on to the treeline and beyond to the distant plain, a blurred abstract in the distance. The further I can see the more of the world there is and the less constricted I feel. The great nothingness gets pushed over the horizon by the eye itself. The longer I can keep looking at it, the more real it becomes. Even if I flew towards that far horizon, I could get no closer. I could stay until day returned to night, just looking, just pushing back the horizon, revelling in the space created, the space between me and the horizon.

To see that the world doesn't exist until consciousness perceives it, is to see the world as enchanted, its existence an aspect of the enchantment of consciousness. But our actions in the material world have consequences we cannot just wish away. I cannot wish away an evil deed simply because I am disgusted by it. I cannot wish away the past, even if I can't see it. No amount of conjuring can change what has already been done. Consequences will roll in and no desperate posturing or frantic imaginings will change that. Fate is but the future we have set up by our past actions, and the actions of those who have come before us. If only I could see the past rising up before my eyes the way I could see the morning landscape unfolding, I would see not only my own life and death but those of my ancestors, and the ancestors of my ancestors all the way back to the birth of suns.

If I didn't know who I was, the ancestors would. They would give me strength and history. Shouldn't they be here to greet me? Familiar hands to guide me into Afterworld, into the great community of death. I felt cheated that there was no welcoming party. No one here to greet me, no angels dressed in robes, no songs of welcome, no outstretched arms. No murmurs of encouragement. Only this mountain, the hut, with flashes of ecstasy and despair.

Maybe those stories about being ushered into Afterworld by friendly hands were nothing more than tales told by the living to drive away the dark.

I had no idea what I had once believed. I didn't know if I was a religious person or a sceptic, a mystic or a practical person. I didn't know how fiercely I identified with my tribe or nation. All I knew was that I was here alone, and that aloneness defined me. It was my boundary.

When no ancestors appeared, I left my vantage point and went searching for my body. I was growing convinced that my body was here somewhere, smashed up on a rock or wedged in a crevasse. If I found it, I would know what age I was, what sex I was. My face, even my dead face, would give me clues as to how I lived, whether I was rich or poor, gentle or bitter, a sower of harmony or discord. If I found my body, if I could perhaps touch it, I might remember. Memory might flow.

The path continued beyond the hut for a bit, then petered out. I searched where I could, in and out of the shadows. I searched in likely and unlikely places. All I found was the whitened skull of an animal. A hare by the look of it. I picked it up and held it in my hands as if it were some precious object. It had eroded away to a few fragile curves of bone. The eye sockets looked huge, too much of the world visible through the gaps. I could feel the hare's fleeting moments as it sprang from tussock to tussock. It lived in a quixotic, ever-changing world. Quivering smells.

In bone is memory, I thought, feeling encouraged. Touching my own bones might bring into memory the life I'd forgotten. Bones are the last to surrender their memories.

With nowhere further to go in that direction, I backtracked past the hut, looking for places where I might have slipped, searching for a sign. I returned along the track that had lead me here, trying to find the spot where I first became conscious of myself, the place where these moments began.

I passed through the grove of beech trees as if through the innards of a woody creature. The beech grove was a single organism. I could hear it breathing. Hear the trickle of its digestion through its fungal roots, the release of mossy odours. Feel its long, slow movement towards the sky. I heard running water, and soon came to a stream so overhung with branches that it was almost hidden. I stopped on the little wooden bridge that spanned it, enchanted by the sound. Like me, the stream didn't know where it had come from or where it was going. These moments sliding over the rocks and slipping under the bridge, unseen by living eyes, were its substance, just as they were mine.

How fragile my briefly created past becomes. As I merge with the sound of the stream, my past tense disappears and all is gathered in this present moment. The movement of water is all about coalescence and release. By emerging from this fictional creation of a past, I can dissolve into this grove of beech and become its substance, from the ragged tips of the trees to the web of its roots. I can feel, not only its respiration but its memories, long slow memories made of minerals and slime, back to when it fought to take root in the rock against the bitter exigencies of the weather.

I diffuse myself through it. I dissolve myself into it. I become nothing but a thin smear of consciousness, an essence without substance. As quick as a thought, a chaffinch swoops by, light and deft. It weaves through the grove like a trick of light. With a rush of wings, a kestrel swoops from between the shadows right through me. I feel its hunger and swift purpose. Silence follows. The shadows fold back into themselves, and I distill myself back into my body. I am once more the spirit-being walking along the path through the beech trees looking for my dead body. Time once more spins its thread, becomes a part of the weave, and I invent the past once more, turn the present into narrative. I am, I was. I was separate once more. In the world but not quite of it.

Where the trail had been washed out, there was a dramatic cliff face, now covered in bright orange lichen. I peered down as if I might see my body lying at the bottom.

On my return, I had the sense of being banished back to the bare rock above the tree line, my little foray into the world of the living being no more than that.

Arriving back at the hut, I hesitated at the door. Night was on the move again, but quietly this time, shadows softly emerging from behind the rocks, the wind no more than a gentle movement of air. The stars were out in all their lucid glory. I had no reason to return to the four walls of the hut. I had no need of its warmth or protection, and yet kept returning to it as if it were a stable reference point.

I had a vision, projected onto the flowing dark of the night sky. A child running through a field of pale-yellow wheat, singing in a voice of heartbreaking purity. I seized upon this as the first genuine memory I'd had since I died. I swooped closer, and soon felt as if I were running alongside the child who began to cover the ground in great leaps. No, not running alongside, flying alongside like a silken bird. I then flew right through the child, through the child's chest, and was left behind in the child's body while the bird flew on.

I am the child. I am the running. That vital force is so strong it lifts me off the ground and sends me running across the sky. I am singing, my voice so pure it comes from beyond my child's body, a voice as pure as feathers are. I go further with each leap, as if I were wearing seven-league boots. I can skip across rooftops. I can jump across valleys from hilltop to hilltop. Over the hills and far away. I can skim the gravity fields of planets. I can jump from creation to creation without turning a hair. I know joy because joy is there to be known. The joy is in the movement, this movement that collapses distances and time.

I might have died as a child. Perhaps I couldn't remember

an adult life because I hadn't had one. This memory of running through the field of wheat could be one of my last memories.

Maybe not, for as soon as I thought this, I saw the child in the back of an old, black car. There were two adults in the front, a man and a woman, with the child alone in the back. The child is playing with the door handle. The door opens the wrong way, so when the wind catches it, it slams open, carrying the child with it. The door handle slips from my grasp, and I fall softly onto the hard road.

I could have died then, on the stony roadside. At that age my sex wouldn't have mattered, which is maybe why I have no stable adult form. I died before I could bud; the future left unformed.

The child lay on the broken stones of the roadside. The brakes of a truck coming up behind squealed. The truck skewed across the road.

I was pleased to have, or so I imagined, something solid to go on. Memories strong enough to be etched against the stars. The mountain sky was still there, like a permanent backdrop. Ragged clouds still rushed across it, carrying stars with them.

But the hut was no longer there. Nestled in the rocks was an old colonial style house facing the road, with a veranda running along the front with wooden lattice-work arching from upright to upright. Surely, I knew this place. There was a large, easy chair on the veranda and in the chair there was an old person. At first I saw this old person from a distance, as if I were passing by on the street. This ancient had grown beyond gender. Even the sex they might have had was a memory.

I shifted from the street into the body of the old person. I was the old person. I am the old person. My vital force is very weak. My blood barely has the strength to circulate. My past tense has faded like an old photograph. My extremities are numb. My head wobbles on top of my shoulders. My hands grip the arm rests like two wizened spiders.

There's a huge face in the sky that might be some god looking down at me. I cling to the world.

It is very hot. From my easy chair I look out onto a road along which a horde of people are moving, shuffling along, all in the same direction. Movements of thought are glutinous. It takes me ages to wonder who all those people are and why they are all moving in the same direction, and why they all look weary and road worn. One of these walkers, they now look like refugees, stops and looks across a bare, windswept yard at me, a child, maybe seven or eight years old, skinny limbed, face etched in hunger. In shame I huddle deeper into my seat, pulling a blanket up around me, an old army blanket smelling of war. It's even hotter inside the blanket, but it affords me a little protection from the eyes of the starving child.

Maybe that was the moment I died, sitting there in that chair, watching all those people shuffling by, huddled under an old army blanket. No, not a chair, a sofa. A place to recline. To lie down and die when the moment comes, the world outside left unresolved, the child paused in its need, a last breath hanging in the air. A god breathing down my neck.

All I had, all I have, is some random images. A child, running into the future. A car door swinging open. An old person sinking through the past. People moving along a road. A starving child. A deity in the wind. These few things projected against the inky night sky before fading back into a trampers' hut and a jumble of rocks. Perhaps I brought these images into being by projecting them, fragments of a movie played against a backdrop of stars. Shifts in thought trigger shifts in perception. I no longer exist, but imagining continues.

I swung from hope to bleak doubt. Glimpses. All I was getting was glimpses, soon erased. Erasure follows me around. My eyes erase everything they see, as the mind erases everything it thinks, the moment of hope, the moment of doubt; the past eroding.

As I moved towards the hut, I began to light up like a Christmas tree. I was in a mature hermaphrodite form, and my body was shifting colours, from green to amber, from brown to ivory and from ivory to purple, a surge from one colour to another, a body created out of a dream of light. There was, there is, no certainty of shape or colour. No settled qualities that cannot be erased. No final definition.

Doubt and uncertainty are the hallmarks of this place. I may know where the cliff edge is, but not what lies beyond it. My feet knew the path to this place. Beyond which there is nowhere to go. When I lie my pretend body down on one of the bunks in the hut, on the lumpy kapok mattress, and look up at the roof, I can see the framing timber and the corrugated iron roof; beyond that, I sense, there is nothing. The hut is floating in a great nothingness.

I reentered the hut after two days away and the mystery of this mundane place deepened, its significance to me undisclosed. When the winds come strong, the hut shakes. It vibrates. Its timbers ache, but it holds fast. It was built to give a little and not to break. Deep piles anchor it to the rock beneath. This rough mountain hut was built to protect fallible mortal flesh. It has a fireplace to warm shivering mortal bodies, mattresses to ease tired mortal flesh and a table at which a living person can sit and eat. I didn't see what use it would be to me. It would go on gathering dust whatever, whereas I am a dustless being. I might as well be outside under a convoy of stars in the vastness of Afterlife. I'm starting to think that I invented the hut, or rather resurrected it from my living days to keep that vastness hidden from me. A shield of tin and wood and crude strength. A place of human connection.

I sat on one of the chairs and stared at the bunks. I had been there before. I had sat at this table. I had slept on one of the bunks, a lower one I believe. And I had not been alone. Another had joined me on that narrow bunk. We had squeezed in together under the old army blanket. We made love. The hut had been flooded with pleasure and abandon. It was a place where I had loved and been loved. The echo of that love anchored me here.

When I lie down on one of the bunks, I lie with a memory. There is room on that narrow bunk for another presence. I can feel the push and pull. Love breathes into my mouth. I breathe into the mouth of love. First I am a man, with all the angelic fury of the male, next I am a woman with all the oceanic swelling of the female. I see-saw back and forth between the two. I become both at the same time, which is neither; I am the push and the pull. The in-breath and the out-breath. I am both the fire and the cauldron out of which the human form emerged. Emerges. Goes on emerging. Resubmerges. Gets erased.

It may be this mortal bliss that connects me now, through the hut, to the land of the living. That connection means that the sun shines and the wind blows, even if the sun rays and the wind pass right though me, turning me into a being of many colours. The semblance of things is maintained. Only if I stare at them for too long do they become transparent.

I believed that there was no fear in Afterworld because fear comes with the body. I believed that freedom from the body meant freedom from fear. Fear is of the body. Fear is for the body. Fear seeks body, embodiment. Anything to which it can cling. A heart to squeeze. Flesh to prickle. A mind to panic.

Fear comes at night with the night wind, a whining at the eaves and windows. As ecstasy fades, I huddle on my bunk and pull up the old army blanket. It smells of fear. It smells of hunger. Alive, you never know when death might strike; dead, you do your best to act as if you are still alive. You are the child who jumped out of the car or the old man letting go on a sofa on a veranda which looked out on a road where hordes of people were moving in one direction, so you lie on a lumpy kapok mattress and pull up a prickly blanket that smells of death around your chin and try to remember love.

I'm terrified that life may suddenly strike like one of the ancient gods, Zeus or Odin, who love to toy with our fates, kill us or bring us to life at will. I could be jarred back into the flesh at any moment. This body could abruptly take being, resolve its uncertainties into a particular form, re-enter gravity. I could find myself alone, naked and shivering in a mountain hut, breathing in the harsh air, once more, back in vertiginous space, my death nothing more than a dream. Random things happen. Perverse things happen. In death, life may lie in wait.

There I was, trapped in a dream of time in a real hut. It was all I had. When I closed my eyes, I could still feel the wooden frame; when I opened my eyes the world was still there, the world of hut and mountain top. The only world I have.

Death is no neutral territory, no passive background, no painted stage set. It's a presence. A presence created by the intensity of absence. Death has a sound. It crackles underfoot like dry grass. It comes in waves like the sound of cicadas. The ordinary mountain sky makes the sound of lots of sticks breaking. I can feel death's breath like a drought on my face and in my lungs. My blood is like dust rustling through my veins. My tongue is caked with it.

It began to rain today. A cold gray light came down from the sky. It swept across the tin roof in gusts, like thousands of little creatures running from one side to the other. Then it came down in earnest, thundering on the roof like a lot of nails being pounded in. I liked it. I was snug and cosy inside while the elements did their worst outside. It made me feel safe, or perhaps allowed me to feel safe. Although I was not cold, I sat on one of the bunks and drew the old army blanket around me and pulled it tight. Now I was safely out of range of the elements. *Snug as a bug in a rug*, someone used to say. I could hear a female voice saying it, soft but clear. That voice had a familiar cadence. That would be my mother, tucking me up in bed at night when I was too young for memories to properly form.

All creatures have a mother. But all I can remember is a train. Where my mother should be there are train tracks, an electric train that flies along at great speed carrying the wind with it. It comes from behind the rain, rattling and crackling as it zooms through the air. The train is not my mother; it is carrying her, taking her far far far away from me, flying away at just under the speed of light. Too fast for my eyes to track, a speed beyond sensation. I feel sad, as when an opportunity has been lost. Sadness is a train carrying everything you love away from you, receding into the distance until it is a tiny point. I feel alone, and not snug as a bug in a rug at all. The train goes into a tunnel and never emerges. The mountain keeps its secrets. The lonesome whistle blows. The tunnel sucks everything into it.

At first I thought the train was empty except for my mother. The train only existed to carry my mother away from me. It had no other purpose. But it turned out that the train was packed with souls, like the famous hell-bound train. Its clattering and clanking merged with the sound of the rain. The wheel of the sky turning, spinning forward and back at the same time as in the movies. Those wheels turn everything, the earth the planets the stars. Movement is headlong. Headstrong. There is no stopping it, no gainsaying it. This train stops at no station. It lets no one off. It is an express. It is heading straight for creation. It bends only with the bending of space. My mother is lost among those lost souls. She is just one among many. Her features are not distinguishable. She has outpaced time. I need to do that too. There must be an art to it. Like the art of getting on a moving train. Half run half leap.

Finally, I grew tired of listening to the rain. It was not taking me anywhere. I was still here and my mother was still far away. It had ceased to be an interesting sound, just noisy. It was not helping me solve the mystery of myself. I decided to get away from it. Perhaps the feel of it on my skin would be enough to awaken something, reclaim something, show me something.

It was wild outside. Driven by contrary winds, the rain surged this way and that. It hit the hut with the force of something solid. But not me. I didn't get buffeted. The rain passed right through me the way sunshine did. I couldn't catch it in my hands or in my mouth. I couldn't taste it. I started to cry. The rain wouldn't wet me, but perhaps my tears would. Perhaps they did. It's hard for me to tell. I was neither wet nor dry. I was outside but I had no inside. This is what it feels like to be dead.

I am not quite separated from things around me, the hut, the mountains, the sky. Where I intersect with the material world there is a fuzziness, a blurring. I don't know where my body ends and the world begins. My feet meet the ground, not with a firm clunk but softly, as if I sink into the ground just a fraction. Same with the wood of the hut, and rock. The sharp edges of the world can't cut me, wound me or bruise me.

As the rain passes right through me I feel a faint tingle as if angels were kissing my skin. Water is mysterious. It shares some properties of the imaginal. It's the only substance that expands as it gets colder. As ice, it creates its own hieroglyphics. Water lives in a manner that remains largely unseen. It enters the body and lives within us. It gives us life and purifies us. If I were a worshipful person, water would be my deity. I've heard that water is everywhere in the universe. There are water molecules hiding in the heart of comets. In this manner it transports itself across the deepest of space.

The rain hardly notices me. I believe there are particles so fine that they can whizz through thick sheets of lead and leave no trace. Neutrinos, that's the word. They hardly register with the material world. So it is with me and the rain. I have to imagine the feel of it in my hair and running over my skin. It is unfair. After all, I can feel the rock of the mountain beneath my feet; I can't walk through the walls of the hut. I am partly of the world. But water is tricky. As it passes through me, those cool pellets penetrating my skin become a part of my substance. Each drop carries its own memories of the sky, the dark clouds from which they are formed, the moment of their separation from the mass, the hurtle earthwards – these memories all became a part of me.

I can open the door of the hut, and close it. I can pick up a small stone, but lack the power to throw it. My state is not consistent; I can't get the better of things. I can hear the wind train but not the sound of my own breath. I can see the mountains but not the lines of my hands. I cling to shreds of wind. My fingers bite into the rock but have no purchase there. I can taste my own mouth but not the astringent rock. Sweet mountain flowers release their scent into my hands, soft as moths. I look out at spring with winter in my hands. I make these words but can't hold onto them. My fingers pass right through them. Words are like the rain. They leapfrog into the air and vanish.

After the rain had washed the sky clean, the moon appeared as if it had jumped into the sky. It was just a bleak piece of rock swinging around the earth, and yet a voice was coming from it, light and cool and shimmering. It came from a far distance, yet was close inside my ear. It sang in my head, an elegy or requiem.

The landscape about me began to twist, flow and change, turning into an open plain scattered with many dead bodies. Their eyes had been pecked by carrion birds. They were mostly soldiers, but mixed in with them were women and some children. Although nothing moved there was no sense of quietude or peace. Pennants moved listlessly. Above them banners of cloud, saturated black, were hoisted into the void. Those starveling dead were shrieking out hunger for their funeral rites. Without their funeral rites they could never leave this battlefield. Unquiet spirits, they would be bound here forever.

'Is that true' I asked the moon, my moon, which was right beside me. It was good to speak words out loud. To let them hang in the air. A faint resonance. These were the first words spoken out loud in Afterlife.

'It is so,' the moon said. 'I sing to lift them but they can't hear me.'

'Could I help? Perhaps offer a libation?'

'Ah,' said the moon, 'You are of good heart. However, the dead need a living person to make a libation. The dead cannot free each other.'

'Oh.' Some scary thoughts began to creep in. The moon could not release me. The earth could not release me. Neither time nor shadows could release me.

'Go with the child,' the moon said.

'What?'

But the moon had lost me amid a chorus of shadows. All I could hear was a faint humming. The battlefield faded.

After I spoke to the moon I saw three chamois.

I am happy to have a sentence like that, even if I am only writing in the air. It doesn't matter if the words don't last much longer than the moment in which they happen; it's what they bring into being that counts. At least some chronology has been established. Something happened, and after that something else happened:

rain, moon and chamois in that order.

I was walking beyond the hut to see what my feet might bring into being, when I heard the clatter of hooves on stone. The path disappeared into a jumble of rock. I came to a precipitous drop. There were three chamois on a peak below me.

It is rare to see these tough goat-antelopes so high up. Their habitat is the alpine fields where they can feed on fresh tussock. There's not much tussock this high. Sturdy looking beasts with the air of mythological creatures, they were leaping from rock to rock with economical movements and some purpose, heading towards, or away, from something.

Unlike me they had somewhere to go.

I watched them for as long as I could. They looked back at me, strange eyes with vertical slits. Their eyes passed over me and I can't be sure they saw me. Maybe they just saw a shadow. They kept looking alertly about, ears pricked up, large eyes wide. They had the look of hunted animals. I wasn't sure if hunters made it up this high.

I didn't know how I would feel if I encountered living, breathing human beings. I didn't know if they would be able to see me. Maybe they would walk right through me and notice nothing. I didn't like that thought. To feel invisible is one thing, even the living can feel invisible, but to actually be invisible is something else again.

Up here, amid the concentrated reality which is bare rock, the idea of warm solvent human flesh seemed quite outlandish. If there were chamois around there could be people. I was the one whose existence was outlandish. Prosaic as they were, they seemed in that moment to be harbingers of the fantastic world of the living and all the creatures who belong to it. They looked fantastic in themselves with their goat faces and deer bodies. They might have stepped out of the pages of a fairy tale.

After they had gone there was nothing left to see but the rocks on which their feet had briefly trod.

My unfinished business with the hut took another turn when I got back to find the hut's visitors' book. I can't understand why I didn't see it before as it was lying on the rough wooden bench that was used as a table. It's old and tatty and dusty, and maybe blended in with the grey dusty table top.

It hadn't been opened for years. The pages were stiff and whispery. It felt odd, looking at it, as if being dead I had no right to pry into the lives of others.

Many of the signatures were illegible, and most of the comments were forgettable. 'I can see for miles and miles and miles...' someone had written. I think that's an old song. 'Stupendous, out of this world,' someone else had written. 'I can breathe,' someone else had written. Lots of exclamation marks everywhere, clusters of them, and big ones with little smiley faces for the dot. 'This is awesome!!!!' or 'Well worth the hike!!!!!!!'

My attention was drawn to one signature. Clear but curly lettering. Ada Camara. She had written, *First there is a mountain then there is no mountain then there is.* That sounded like an old song too. I knew the name, Ada Camara. It stood out from all the others. It resonated with me. It was a clue, if only I knew how to read it. Hers were big, generous, roundy letters. I ran the name over in my mind. As I did so I seemed to fall into a state of reverie, imitating sleep.

Do the dead sleep? That seems like a silly question given that death is seen as eternal sleep, but I know now that death is not eternal sleep but rather eternal wakefulness. What I experience as sleep is the feeling of being at one remove from that wakefulness. There, thought is carried lightly in the mind which, untethered, can wander freely between life and death.

The dead dream of life, like bright feathers in the morning light.

I dreamed of a woman named Ada Camara, a woman who would sign her name like that. She was African black, deep black. Like the mountain sky. Her lips were wide. Her skin the texture of linen. Hers was a fierce beauty, a living force that animated the world around it.

My heart staggered in my chest. We were sitting at a window table in a busy restaurant. It was an upmarket restaurant with manufactured art work on the walls. The table cloth was very white. I could see faint lines where the folds had been ironed. A jug of water sat between us. We each had a glass of water in front of us. Slight ripples occurred on the water, a blurred texture, as if far beneath us some mighty engine was labouring away.

All around us people came and went, chattering blithely and balancing cups of coffee and plates with delicacies, but Ada and I were silent. Nobody took any notice of us. Everybody else was talking or consulting their cellphones but I couldn't make out any words. We didn't eat anything and only drank sips of water. Apparently, we were waiting for something. Or somebody. Whatever it was I didn't want it to come. I wanted to hold back time. I wanted the moment in the restaurant to never end.

A waitress came up to our table. Surely, we needed something. No, we didn't. She had long fingers, with the nails peeling off, showing pink skin beneath.

Outside the window, hordes of people were passing, all in the same direction, looking neither right nor left but eyes fixed on the ground in front of them. There was an ancient weariness in them. As we watched, one of the walkers fell over, a bundled layer of rags. A few people stopped and bent over the fallen form while others walked around them or pushed past. I could tell that this person was dead; it was the way they fell, the finality of it. Somebody dragged the body to one side of the pavement and those who had stopped kept walking. Nobody in the restaurant was taking any notice, as if the walkers didn't exist. Their chatter never ceased.

A child among the walkers stopped to look in. Her hair was matted and her face was streaked with dirt. She stared at Ada and me, and at our jug of water. Suddenly our jug of water was no ordinary thing. The clean water shone with extraordinary purity. We could see the world through it.

'It's not working out,' Ada said. She had a deep, smooth contralto.

I didn't know what she was talking about. I looked around the restaurant as if I could find some answers there. The waitress with peeling fingernails was serving the table across from us. Somebody was ordering wine. A child was eating ice-cream. It looked like things were working out for some people.

'Nobody has to die,' Ada said. Her voice was thrilling. It vibrated right through my body. 'You're not going to die.' From the way she said that, I knew she loved me. She didn't want me to die. I was happy about that. If I meant something to this magnificent woman, then my life had not been completely wasted.

The child with the matted hair disappeared from the window, swept away by the shuffling crowd.

'But someone has just died,' I said. I could taste ash in my mouth. It was acrid. 'There is a body in the street.'

'There's more than one,' Ada said.

The child eating ice-cream began to cry.

I was full of dread, not for myself but for Ada. This was not her place. This was a city of death. There was nothing but hard walls and hard pavements. And rich people in restaurants. The wilds would have suited her better, yellow grassy plains where her beauty could reign unhindered. Those same wheat fields through which I had run as a child would have suited her better. Any open place. Something terrible was going to happen to her, and I could do nothing to stop it. I lacked any power or agency. My mouth could find no words.

We just sat there waiting for it to happen. We could only watch and wait and look at each other and take sips of water.

From far off, we heard the sound of artillery. Big guns booming distantly, coming closer. The woosh-boom of missiles. The horde of people on the road were fleeing, but lacked the strength to do more than drag themselves along. Distant doors were slamming, the horizon contracting. Nobody had to die but people were dying nevertheless.

Someone appeared in the doorway, lit from behind. A tall figure with wings of shadow. While I couldn't make out any features, I was convinced that this silhouette was the angel of death. It was the look on Ada's face, the stiffening of her body, all that beauty clenched like a fist.

Slowly the plate glass of the restaurant began to blow inwards with great force. Shards of glass went flying, slicing into the flesh of people at their tables. Ada and I were right by the window. We were the first to go.

Abruptly, I found myself back in the hut. I was sitting at the table, the visitors' book in front of me, a hard morning light coming through the window. The guns had fallen silent; the road emptied into the stars. On the veranda, an old person drew their last breath. The child who could jump from mountain top to mountain top fell out of the back of a car. A star fell into a ravine. Only the chamois witnessed the fall. The restaurant faded in a hail of light.

Ada and I had often dined at that restaurant. Sometimes she flirted with the waitress with peeling fingernails and I got jealous. It felt as if there were two realities meshed together, the restaurant and its heedless customers and the street outside where refugees fled from approaching war. These fragments didn't quite fit.

It pleased me to think that I might have died in Ada's warm presence. She had a beautiful singing voice, rich and tremulous. She could sing the famous aria from Tosca 'Vissi d'arte,'

I lived for my art, I lived for love,
I never did harm to a living soul!

I have just these few images of her. Nothing more. No connective tissue, no temporal sinews.

The further I thought my way into this, the less certain I became. I was a tiny fragment of a shattered plate-glass window. The deeper I burrowed into the details, the less I understood the overall picture, even as the blood was flowing, even as the screams were fracturing the air.

Just a few moments ago, it seems, I saw Ada again. We are walking arm in arm down a deserted main street looking into shops. We are the only living souls there. The food bars are deserted, their counters attended by lines of empty chrome stools, stiff and silent. There is no food in the display units. ATM machines blink sleepily. There are human figures like reflections mysteriously left behind in the glass of shop windows after the original images have long since moved on. Those images continue their shadow life.

The windows portray different aspects of home life. There are kitchens, living rooms and bathrooms. There are people dressed in freshly pressed clothes doing commonplace things like cooking in a kitchen with sparkling new appliances, watching big-screen tv in a living room reeking of newness, and cleaning their teeth in spangly bathrooms. There is an outdoor scene showing a barbecue in a backyard. Mannequins stand about with their smug blind eyes and smart attire, holding glasses perpetually half full. A couple of kids with white socks play tag. Their shorts have clean, sharp creases. Had there been a dog somewhere, it would have barked. Only when one of these figures move do I realize that they are real people acting out the frozen gestures of mannequins.

We don't linger. We are there to be together, walk together. Admire each other, our fine female forms. Ada looks spectacular in a tank-top and shorts. I am wearing a peasant blouse with ruffled sleeves and a pleated skirt. We look quite wonderful. We feel quite wonderful. She is black and I am hot pink. There are some moments in life you could die for, when you have never felt closer to the world. Even the pretend mannequins in the window notice us, and peer out at us as if we were the ones on display.

I take hold of Ada's arm as the tank comes around the corner. The pretend mannequins hide their faces. The tank's turret swings back and forth in an evil manner. Its slender barrel points right at us. It is like a little round, black eye.

I am grateful to have known such love when I was alive. What greater doom is there to die without a love such as Ada Camara and I had walking down that main street with the shiny windows?

Sitting with the book in front of me, I noticed another signature, one that piqued my curiosity. A name was coming in and out of focus, the signature changing shape as I looked at it. Could the signature be mine? That was an intriguing possibility. Perhaps I would find out my name at last, my mark in the world. The emerging signature was familiar, like something I had lived with. Names flowed in and out of one another without solidifying.

Staring at that signature, I saw a tall man. He had broad shoulders, long arms and long, supple fingers, a musician's fingers. He was stooping to pick something up. It was a large, gray river stone. It was heavy and he was struggling. I felt immensely sorry for him, a pity so all-encompassing it could swallow me up. I wanted to warn him that the stone was too heavy, that it would tear the heart out of his chest if he tried to lift it. I wanted to tell him not to put too much faith in his physical strength, that his physical strength was an illusion.

I knew that if he succeeded in picking up the stone it would be the last thing he ever did. I might have been that man, about to lift a weight too heavy for my heart to bear. I sensed in him a life dedicated to others. A death in the service of others. The stone he was attempting to lift was not his own.

I saw his funeral. He was in a tall coffin. I walked behind the coffin, my feet as heavy as two stones. A child, her head held high, walked beside me, her face carefully composed. She was dressed in black, and fully up to the solemnity of the occasion. I smiled at her encouragingly. 'In the midst of life we are in death,' the presiding minister intoned as we stood around the grave. It started to rain. Ada was there too. She wore a dark shawl over her face. In a voice slow and deep, she was singing to herself in a language I didn't know. Slowly the grave was filling up with water. The gray sky was reflected in it. As the water rose, it lifted the sky with it. The coffin sank.

The signature turned into a name. Wilson Harris. He was the tall man, the man with long, flexible fingers. He had been a cartographer, map maker, explorer and connoisseur of wild places. He'd come to the hut on some official business that had to do with surveying. I saw him sitting at this very table, surrounded by the instruments of this trade, a slide-rule, a set square, a protractor, a theodolite, and maps. He was so deep in thought it was dripping from his forehead. He was focused on organising what he could see in his mind's eye, taming the wild peaks and cliffs to lines on the page. This was his work, what he loved to do. He had dedicated his life to reducing three dimensions to two.

'I am king of all I survey,' he had written beside his signature. With a smiley emoji. I could see the wry smile on his face when he wrote those words.

He'd also done a curious little doodle showing what could be a set of steps, or a piano keyboard. A little stairway going nowhere.

For a heady moment, I thought I had found myself. That I was Wilson Harris, the cartographer, the tall man. That gave me something. A substance. An identity. A name. A job. And, finally, a settled gender. It even gave me a probable cause of death.

Yet, I had been to the funeral. Not my own funeral, for I had walked behind his coffin in the company of a child. I had watched the sky pour into his grave. Heard the hard breathing of the mourners.

Wilson Harris had been my friend, I thought, perhaps more than a friend. We had been up here together. I saw his somewhat dour face close to mine in flickering firelight. I felt his delicate hands in mine. I heard his voice which was deep and sepulchral. Or, he might have been my father. I couldn't rule that out. He'd died when the weight of the world grew too much for him to bear.

That I had no way of distinguishing between these equally plausible alternatives was frustrating. I was coming to understand that the more I saw, the less I knew for certain. This is how it was going to be. My struggle had been futile all along. My natural desire to know who I was and how I died had led me to this place where some common elements, like Ada, the child, the restaurant and the people on the road, the tall man, the old man on the veranda, kept getting moved around and re-presented in changing contexts. On every side the landscape falls away.

After flicking through it from the beginning, I slammed the visitors' book shut with a bang. Dust flew up from the pages. Angels danced briefly in the dust. All the 'awesomes' were a bit nauseating. 'I'm the king of the castle and you're all dirty rascals' is all I was seeing in those entries. If I thought I was going to find any clues about the circumstances of my life and death, I was mistaken. I discovered Ada and Wilson Harris, and had some pictures in my head that seemed to fit the names. Nothing more.

It had been a fool's errand to begin with.

I heard a piano playing. I was lying on the bunk, trying to remember my life, trying to remember something I could rely on, thinking about Ada and the tall man, when I heard Bach's C Major Prelude from *The Well-Tempered Clavier*. Soft, rapid notes played with confidence. There was a beautiful clarity in it, in both the music and the playing. Somehow it was simple and complex at the same time; simple in construction, complex in affect. It resounded in the hut as if in a large auditorium, but the sound was coming from outside. In the precise arrangement of notes, there emerged stars and solar systems. The music of the spheres. I've heard that phrase. Music is spherical. It takes place in three-dimensional space, but is born beyond spacetime. It starts as a single note, which is replicated and refracted through the lens of spacetime. Our ears make sense of it. It is transmitted through the body's nervous system.

I followed the sound, or tried to, looking futilely for a piano. As if there was going to be a concert grand tucked away behind a crag or in the shadow of a rock, maybe from a crevasse somewhere, made of Sitka spruce, the most resonant wood in the world. Amazing the way wood can carry sound. This playing was connected to Wilson Harris. A cartographer of melodies, perhaps, whose long subtle fingers were made for the keyboard.

I didn't find anything. But the music continued. It boomed out of the rocks; it poured forth from the sky. It was everywhere and nowhere. I gave myself over to it. Quickly and easily, it obliterated me. I became a sequence of notes. I tripped lightly from one to the next. Up and down the staircase I went. I lingered where there was resonance. I hurried where there was urgency. I paused where there was a beat. There was no me, just the quickening of the tempo of consciousness. An emergent melody beyond thought. Alive, I had a body I could never entirely leave behind, not even in the midst of the highest transports, with this body, however, put together out of momentary imaginings, there were no impediments. I evaporated in an instant. I was the music, both its expression and its underlying structure. I was each individual note, and I was the melody. As the music, I was able to create realms, extensions of space made possible by the disclosure of beauty. This music did not happen within time, it created time. It created the time in which it could have its being. It was a form of life. It was my blood.

Then it stopped. The last note soared over the edge of silence, and was gone. The time and space it had created for its existence shrank to an infinitesimal point, and vanished. I was back on the mountainside, half in and half out of the shadow of a rock. I reappeared as a child. I sat at a piano. Somebody was standing behind me, a looming adult presence, teaching me how to play.

I didn't have long, skinny fingers. Rather, short, stubby ones. Those stubby fingers didn't know where to go. Notes fell all over the place. There was a piano teacher but I couldn't see her. She was hiding behind her voice which was hiding behind me. When I turned around all I saw was the rocky mountainside. I was having trouble coordinating my left and right hands. I was embarrassed about my clumsy body. My clumsy hands. My little sausage fingers that dangled from my hand. The keyboard was huge. On either side of me, it disappeared off into the distance.

'I've got to meet Pip soon,' I said.

The piano teacher said something soothing.

'Pip will be waiting' I said.

But my fingers had to do some more froggy jumps.

Those notes too faded slowly, and there was no sound other than the wind and the occasional scuttle of rock. The empty ringing sound the sky makes.

The dead don't kick up much of a fuss. But there are voices, I realized, an unseen choir, a cacophony of voices. In that maelstrom there is every possible human utterance. The background hum of human consciousness. You don't have to hear it. Your own consciousness is a part of it. I take no notice of it. If I think about it too much, I start to go a little crazy. There are so many voices, swelling and fading, my own becomes meaningless.

Since I'm in an inaccessible mountain hut on an inaccessible mountain, as high as I can get without leaving the planet, it's natural to assume that I am alone. For me, being dead is about aloneness. Sometimes that frightens me. I become a child. My emotions are as sudden and overwhelming as a child's. To be alone means to cry in the dark. Sometimes however it excites me. Only when I am alone can I fully be myself, with an expansion of being in which there is no horizon. Whatever I might be feeling, whether breathing deep or shallow, I take aloneness to be my essential condition. The dead do not keep each other company.

Sometimes, however, I sense there are others here with me. I can't see them or touch them, but feel them with my mind. They are the unseen choir. They hover beyond the boundaries of thought. They are inside my hut, and they are out on the mountain side too. Even the sky is packed with them. Maybe the whole universe. Even in the deepest of deep space you can hear their descant. I don't think they are any more aware of me than I am of them. Some come close. We are like the proverbial ships in the night. A shadow passing. We are known only by the waves we make. Only the ripples created by our wake overlap. Only the background hum remains.

Knowing this is no comfort. I am still alone. I cry in the dark, friendless and uncomforted. The more I sense the presence of these others, the more alone I feel. At times I'm spooked by their voices, their omnipresent laments There is some humour in that, a dead person feeling spooked, but this is spooky as love can be spooky. Love is spooky because there is something otherworldly about it. Something beyond our comprehension. To be loved is to be touched by another, by the other. I take these others with me everywhere I go, and they do the same with me.

Sometimes I feel myself being carried along. Being taken to places I've never been before, cities and landscapes, streets and markets. In such moments I am somebody else's invisible presence, and that makes me uncomfortable. Some unsuspecting soul, engaged in an everyday, mundane activity, shivers, even in the hot sun, and is reminded of their mortality.

Sometimes I weep because I sense a love that was never mine, a love that I never knew. A love I might have yearned for, a love others have known. I don't want to get myself mixed up with the memories of other dead people, their loves and their lives. I just want to know about my own. I dread ending up not knowing who I am or where I am, or how I might escape. I am coming to believe that when I know how I died I will know how to escape from here. I will be able to find my way off this mountainside.

Sometimes I resent these others. They are trespassers. What right do they have to intrude? Surely the dead are entitled to some privacy, especially up here. A mountain top is no place to feel hemmed in.

Recently, I discovered that I was not alone. I'm not talking about the shadowy, displaced voices who crowd around and are packed into every available space. Their existence is notional. They lie at a tangent to my perceived world. Rather, I sensed someone just like me, of the same substance. Another dead person. I had company just when I thought I had none. Someone else wanted to share my mountain fastness.

It started with the sound of a human voice, a child's voice. A child singing. Not singing so much as keening, a long sad sound in a high register. At first I thought it was nothing more than the wind in mourning. Then I heard a sob that could have come only from a human throat, for while the wind can ululate, it cannot sob.

I was lying on a bunk looking up at the tin roof when I heard it. My immediate thought was that it was a memory of some kind. I was eager for memories, and seized on it as some new clue. When I heard the sound being blown around by the mountain wind, I got up and slipped outside. The wind was light and gusty, and it was an exceptionally clear night. In a perfectly cliched way, the stars looked like a trove of jewels in a giant's treasure chest. Or a dragon's. They shimmered with colours I didn't recognise. I could easily find my way. In their constellations, I could see the outline of a woman, naked to the waist, pouring water from a pool onto parched land.

'Hello,' I called.

The voice stopped.

There was no one in sight. I walked around the hut and saw nothing out of place.

'Coming ready or not,' I called.

A giggle.

'I'll find you.'

I crept around the crag, hoping to catch them unawares. I became a child, a little boy, maybe nine years old, playing hide and seek or some such game. Catch me if you can! Around the other side of the rock, away from the hut, I found her. We stared at each other. She was also about nine years old and had huge dark spaces where her eyes should be. Her hair was long, and appeared silver in the starlight.

A person in bare feet. A dead person just like me. Like me, her skin kept changing colour all the time, but in the starlight it just turned from silver to gray and gray to coal as if clouds were passing overhead.

I was ambivalent about sharing my space up here. I was remote, out of range, alone, alone forever and always no matter how hard that was. You die and then you are alone. That's how it works, or how I thought it worked. This is my death, and mine alone. Or so I thought.

Another dead person around complicated what was beautifully simple. Before it was very clean. Just me, the mountaintop, the hut and all it contained. And pictures cast against the inky night sky, the mind's own aurora. With the arrival of another, that simplicity was lost. Being dead was no longer a straightforward, personal matter. I remember a story once about a man washed up on an island who lived alone for many months and came to accept aloneness as his condition before, one day, finding a footprint in the sand that was not his own.

I understand how he felt. Solitude was no longer his defining condition. No matter how bare the rock and how pitilessly the mountain wind blew and how dark the night became, this was my irremediable condition, my mystery. Until now.

'Do you want to come inside?' I said. My voice had a plaintive edge. I gestured to the open door of the hut.

Her first response was terror, as if I was the angel of death about to drag her off to hell. I smiled encouragingly and made no move. Eventually, she nodded. It was a lonely nod. I became sad, wished I was an adult again. I needed to be an adult to understand that kind of sadness mixed with pity that percolates over a lifetime. As a nine year old I could only guess at it, feel the edges of it.

I was very protective of this huddled child in an adult way. She looked like one of those children who grew old before her time.

She hung around the door, fearful, peering into the darkness of the hut.

'It's okay inside,' I said. 'It's just a hut. It's...familiar.'

'Familiar?' She took the necessary steps, one courageous step after another. Crossing the threshold was a difficult moment for her. I had no idea how long she'd been out there, but it seemed being outside had become natural to her. With reluctance she passed into the shadow of the hut.

Inside, she looked around in wonder, perhaps at the very ordinariness of things. I wondered what she could see with those pits for eyes, but didn't ask. Finally, she lingered on the empty fire grate. She sat in front of it and rubbed her hands. I understood. Just because fire can't warm your body doesn't mean it can't warm your soul. I built a fire. There was a pile of firewood I could use. It was old and dry. I carried it to the grate and found some matches beside the woodpile. They lit easily, as if waiting for the opportunity to flare into life.

Satisfied, we held our hands up to the flames but felt nothing. To show off, I held my hand over the flame, in the flame. I thought of the original fires of creation out of which our bodies were forged. I did feel something. A tingling far off as if I had nerves extending beyond my body.

I showed the little girl how to do it and we both held our hands in the flame and felt a far-off tingling. The flames were reflected in the dark spaces of her eyes. They seemed to burn inside her head. She smiled. She had lovely teeth. Her smile made me sad, and I didn't want to be sad because I might become an adult again. Adults are the saddest.

We pretended the fire was warming us. Pretending was almost as good as the real thing. We both wanted to laugh. So we did. We toasted our little toes as if they were marshmallows and laughed some more. Once we did toast marshmallows like this over a real fire, and life was a sweet taste in our mouths. This little girl and I had known each other when we were alive, I was sure of that. We'd played and had fun together, told stories and eaten marshmallows around a fire. We had been companions. Perhaps she'd been my sister, my twin, my other face. There had to be a reason she'd turned up, her arrival no coincidence.

Then I noticed her clothes. They were poor and ragged. She looked like the little match girl in the Hans Anderson fairy tale. Her arms and legs were thin and her face small. Her hair was dark, tapering into rattails. I sensed that she'd died in those clothes. They were all she had to die in. She'd died on the road, a refugee, abandoned and forgotten, without a funeral, without proper rites, a pale child of the moon. My heart went out to her. I wanted to make up for all the kindness she'd never received in her lifetime.

'What's your name?' I asked her. I rolled the familiar phrase around in my mouth as if it were an exotic language. And it was. It was the language of living creatures, not a good fit for the mouths of the dead.

She shook her head. She was trying to fit words into her mouth too; her tongue was searching for their shape. 'I don't know.' It was a child's voice. A small voice in a huge universe of remote, moving things. My voice sounded the same. Small and childlike. We had nothing but this little hut and a fire that couldn't warm us.

'Maybe your name was Pip.'

'How do you know?'

'I don't, I just thought...' I didn't know what I thought. I couldn't shake the feeling that someone called Pip had been waiting for me.

'We don't have names,' she said, and again after a pause, 'that's not fair.'

'It's not,' I said. 'Everybody has a name.'

Without a name I felt abandoned. Both of us. Nameless and forgotten.

'Even my dog had a name,' she said. 'Mooch. He would eat poo.'

We thought about how funny it was that she could remember her dog's name but not her own.

'I think it was our dog,' she said.

'How did you die?'

'I don't know.'

I didn't feel too disappointed. I hadn't expected anything. She was in the same position I was in. That is, nowhere at all.

'How did you die?' she said.

'I don't know.' Maybe I also died without my proper rites. Maybe that's why we were both here. Without our funeral rites we might be abandoned in this place of lost souls, just as the moon had said. Battlefield survivors, so lost we couldn't find our own graves.

She nodded. 'Are you sure we're dead? If we're dead, how can we be talking like this?'

I nodded. 'I'm sure. It's the one thing I am sure of. We can produce shadow words. Nothing more.' And that's all they are, I thought. Shadow words which have no agency in the real world.

She nodded. We nodded together. 'I'm sure too. Dreams aren't like this.'

'Have you been here before? I mean, to this hut? When you were alive?'

She hesitated. 'I think so. What about you?'

'I'm sure I was. That's why I'm here. I think.'

'You don't remember?'

'Not exactly. I'm not even sure we can remember things. I mean...the way living people do. It's different for us.' All we have are shadow memories, I thought. Memories without substance. Not remembering made me feel small and useless. I wanted to be an adult so I could remember adult things, but that didn't work. I stayed a child. I struggled to find any adult feelings. All I could taste was marshmallows, and the loneliness of the youngest child, the one that's always left behind. The one that never gets the last marshmallow.

The girl looked at me with pity. Despite her age, she knew how vast the night was. In a maternal gesture, she put her arm over my thin shoulders. 'How you lived is all that matters,' she said. 'Were you kind to others?' The question was important to her, I felt, because like the little match girl she hadn't known much kindness in her short life.

As she spoke I saw a dog, a dachshund, sitting by the fire looking up at her with that yearning look that dogs get sometimes. Mooch, I thought.

'I don't think so,' I said. I don't know why I said that, because I didn't have a clue how I lived, I just sensed that if I had been kind to others, I wouldn't feel so small and scared and lost and lonely. I'd feel big and confident and grown up, able to face my death squarely. Or I'd still be feeling that ecstasy that I felt earlier and none of this childish stuff would matter. The cosmos would take over and that would be it, I would leap over the sky and be gone.

'I think you were,' she said.

'Why?'

'Because you are now.'

I understood that. If I'd been cruel in my life, how could I be kind in Afterworld? Death cannot bring about a moral transformation. At the same time, I became convinced that she was thinking of someone else, that she looked at me with those pits for eyes and saw someone else. But I wouldn't disappoint her by telling her so. That would be mean.

'Are you always a little girl?'

She looked puzzled.

'I mean...I'm a boy now, with you, but mostly I'm an adult. I became a boy when I was looking for you. Sometimes I'm a man, sometimes a woman, sometimes...both.'

She shook her head. 'I've always been a little girl, but I'd like to be grown up. If I could be a woman.'

I saw the woman she'd like to be, her hair bushed blonde across her shoulders. Her arms long and supple. Her laughter as sweet as a field of yellow flowers. This was her way of being grown up.

'I think that means you died as a child, I mean the age you are now.'

'How do you know?'

'Because you can't be an adult. You have no adult form.'

'And you do?'

'Yes.'

'Show me, then. Be an adult. I want to see you.'

'Ok.'

I tried. I tried very hard. I remembered Ada. Ada and I walking down a street looking into the shops resplendent in our adult forms. Nothing happened. I remained a child, a little boy, just the way the girl saw me. I tried to feel very adult feelings, but everything I felt, even my love for Ada, the little boy could feel. I felt a touch of panic. I didn't mind being a little boy, but didn't want to stay that way forever just because that's the way I looked to her.

'I can't. Maybe it's the kind of thing you can't do when you're trying.'

'Or maybe you only think you can.'

'There is a woman, Ada.'

'Who's Ada?'

Maybe nothing more than a signature in a visitors' book, I thought.

'I think Ada and I were sort of married. And I had a friend, a man called Wilson Harris.'

'I had a dog,' she said.

We sat in silence, and the silence grew hopeless. We knew nothing, that was the truth of it. The past can't anchor the dead the way it does with the living; we can look at something for a long time and not see it. I thought because we were together we must have known each other in our lives, but when I searched her face for some clue, something I might remember, I saw only the vacancies that were her eyes. I saw nothing. Emptier than a starless night. I realized that when she looked at me, she must see the same thing. We were two emptinesses looking at each other. Looking for answers that weren't there.

When the fire died down I put on more wood. We sat there without knowing what to say. The silence turned our minds into echo chambers.

'It's all so familiar, I'm sure I used to come up here,' I said. 'I used to come up here a lot, as an adult. Maybe I was a scientist, studying the moss, lichens and liverworts. I think it was the one place in the world where I was truly happy. There is true happiness and untrue happiness. There are masks of happiness. That's why I came here when I died. I returned to the place with which I had the strongest connection.' That sounded right to me. And since I had nothing else to go on, sounding right was good enough. Sound enough.

While I had been saying these things I had grown up again. I had taken on my adult form, and I had grown up female. My funeral suit had become a long black gown, hemmed in white lace. I was beautiful and celestial. My hair bushed into the light. My arms grew long and sinuous. I looked like the woman the little girl wanted me to be, half human half goddess but in fact neither. My pity for the ragged little girl turned into compassion. That compassion was deep enough to hold the world itself. I suddenly yearned to take flesh again, to become a real person, to fill out this wonderful body with real blood, in visceral space, warm and throbbing. I wanted to be alive.

The girl watched me with astonishment. 'I wish I could do that,' she said. 'It's not fair.'

I wanted to gather the child into my arms and soothe away her distress. 'There's a reason you're here with me,' I said, my voice as low and soft as the dying fire, 'I just don't know what it is.'

She said, 'My family used to bring me here. That was before the war. It was a long time ago. I had a mother. And a father. And a dog. And some uncles and aunts. And some cousins I didn't see very often. I think most of them were killed in the war.'

As she spoke, I became less sure that we had occupied the same era when alive, or even the same world. For all I knew, she might have come from another earth, a parallel world across the fault lines of time. Or she might have been remembering a previous life. I thought of that because she spoke as if she were very old. An ancient voice was coming out of that's child's mouth, a voice steeped in war.

I didn't know what war she was referring to, but was reminded of the restaurant, the sounds of war approaching, the plate glass window exploding inward. There are layers of time, undulating membranes sliding over each other. Worlds over worlds.

We sat that way, not saying much, until the second lot of wood had faded to a dim glow. Silence blossomed in the empty grate. Then it was time to rest. The dead don't need to rest, but do so anyway, out of habit as much as anything else. To lie down and close your eyes remains a peaceful thing to do. The dead can't sleep but we can dream. The dreams of the dead are lucid.

At that moment, just as we were about to leave the fireplace, we both felt another presence in the room. We looked at each other in consternation and slowly turned our heads towards the doorway. The door was open and blue starlight flowed into the room. Standing at the threshold there was silhouetted a human-shaped figure. A being was standing there, unmoving, a being that was darkness layered upon darkness. A darkness so deep and vast it contained everything, all bright and living things. It had no settled form, seething and coiling tendrils of shadow only. Because it held everything within it, it was aware. It was aware of us, we were a part of its all-encompassing nature. I had seen this being before, at the restaurant just before it exploded, standing in the doorway, the light flaming behind it.

And it was here for a reason. We were the reason.

We knew that it was waiting, and what it was waiting for. It was waiting for us. Looking at it, yet wanting to shield my eyes from that darkness, I knew with the certainty of dread that my time on the mountainside, in this hut, was running out. I might clutch at a few images from my life, search for the flare of narrative, locate a few memories, but there was no holding onto them. Death awaited at that wooden threshold with its final promise – all would be gathered up and subsumed by those membranes of darkness.

'You have brought the end with you,' I said to the child.

'And you brought me here,' she said.

'I only died a few moments ago,' I said.

'Me too,' she said

'There's no duration here,' I said. 'Everything's happening at once.'

She nodded solemnly, like a very old person. 'This is our last real place,' she said.

I am walking along a road with many others. The heat is intense. I am wracked by hunger and thirst. The dust beneath our feet is thirsty. My sandals are falling apart. My feet are bleeding. Only my will keeps me going. My will is ageless, my body is not. My body wants to die. Only the refusal to die keeps me going. When I started out with all the others, I thought I was going to a better place. A place where a person could live a decent human life free from fear and oppression and the imminence of war. Now I no longer believe it. Hope has been ground underfoot by our shuffling feet. Resentment so deep it has turned into hatred possesses me. I hate those who have done this to me, who have pushed me onto this road. Who are steadily pushing me, and others around me, to my death. My death is not far off. Like the distant mountains, it grows closer with every step. It once seemed far away. Now I am in the foothills. Gravity bears me down.

I watch birds fall dead out of the air, and fruit broil on the branch from the heat – and I stagger from the shame of it. I hate what the warmongers have done to our world, turning it from green pastures to dust or mud, the same dust that now clogs our broken feet. The same mud in our mouths when we try to talk. This is a war against everything, everything that lives and moves and breathes and loves. The war will only end when there is nothing left. Not a blade of grass. Not a single creeping insect. Not a bird. Until there is nothing but negation.

When I look at the mountains now looming closer, I imagine cool beech forests and swarming streams. I see the swift falcon and the shy fern bird. I see a velvet night sky in which the cosmos turns. I imagine a mountain hut, nestled in the rocks, far away from all this, from the dust and the thirst and the killing road. A place where death will feel comfortable. Hell is no place to die.

All around me, the moaning of souls in torment. I try to shut my ears to them. The moaning comes from near and far. From the four directions. It swells and subsides like a miserable tide. I cry out, perhaps in an effort to block out the others, but my voice merges with theirs, my cry just one among many.

I hold my head up high so I don't have to look at the shuffling dust. It feels heavy on my thin shoulders. It can only tip forward.

Distant helicopters, their chopping coming and going in the wind, are slowly drawing near.

I shifted from that vision to the hut, and music in my head, some orchestral piece complete with swirling strings. I didn't recognise it. It came and went as if an orchestra were playing outside in the wind.

I struggled to understand. Did I die on the road? Fall over into the dust? Get shot from a helicopter? There are countless ways to die. Perhaps to die one death is to die all of them.

Many of us die on our roads to a vision of a place. Some appear to have somewhere to go; some are moving while others stand still and let the road do the walking. We struggle to maintain a meaningful context. I don't so much want to know how I died as how I lived. I want to know if I was an honourable person. If I respected my family and my ancestors, honoured my lineage. The dead are very concerned about their honour. Since wealth is quite meaningless to us, the old saying you can't take it with you is perfectly true, we are left with little else but honour, our self-respect, our histories.

How we lived is more important to us when we're dead than when we're alive. That's because when we're alive we think that other things are more important, like money and power and sex. And there's always a future. If you don't like who you are, you can take action. You can shape your fate with your hands. Dead, you have no power over the world, man or beast, or anything crawling between heaven and earth. You can't change anything. You can scratch at the world and not leave a single mark.

The idea that you have dominion over anything fades faster than flesh. Your dispossession is immediate. Your power is stripped away. You can no longer kill, or bring to life. You may be in the world but not of it.

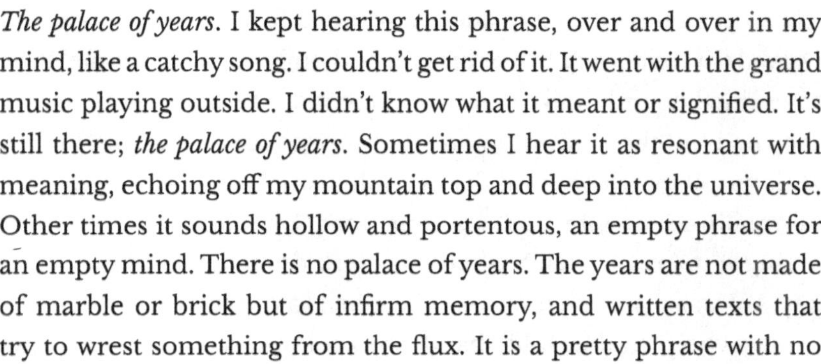

The palace of years. I kept hearing this phrase, over and over in my mind, like a catchy song. I couldn't get rid of it. It went with the grand music playing outside. I didn't know what it meant or signified. It's still there; *the palace of years.* Sometimes I hear it as resonant with meaning, echoing off my mountain top and deep into the universe. Other times it sounds hollow and portentous, an empty phrase for an empty mind. There is no palace of years. The years are not made of marble or brick but of infirm memory, and written texts that try to wrest something from the flux. It is a pretty phrase with no substance, its resonance imaginary.

Afterworld is one of those words. It sounds mysterious, if not a little grandiose. One imagines all kinds of things. Clouds pretty with palaces. Clouds festooned with hierarchies of song. Or a land of smudgy darkness. In fact, there is no afterlife, so there is no afterworld. I don't have any kind of world, before or after. I don't even have a concrete shape, since my body can change with a change in the wind or a current of feeling. I imagine myself as a dead branch around which the wind will curve, but even that dead branch has a shape. It can make a silhouette against the morning sky. I can't do that. I can't make a silhouette against anything. The sun's rays pass right though me. The dead have no shadow.

So the music will go on playing in the Palace of Years. I think it might be Holst's *The Planets*. Mars, perhaps. Swirling and portentous. Like war.

Nothing like this simple hut, or the two lost souls that inhabit it.

There was a time the child and I descended from the mountain and walked through a city full of bridges and buildings and people. Bare trees lined the sidewalk. They had done more than lose their leaves, they had lost their souls. No one took any notice of us. Dogs looked at us suspiciously because they couldn't smell us. I was hiding my hermaphrodite state under a long coat. I couldn't risk anybody seeing who I really was. My body was forbidden in the streets of this city. If I was discovered, I would be taken to the surgeons.

I was holding the child's hand. She kept squeezing it as if to make sure I was still there. We were frightened. The city was frightening because it was no longer ours. Because we no longer belonged in it. Because it no longer belonged to us. We no longer recognised it, and it no longer recognised us. The city was a place for scurrying, death-bound creatures, all running, consumed by various hungers. First in one direction, then the other. Surging back and forth, in and out of buildings. They had no time to recognise each other. Everybody with something to do and somewhere to go. Everybody looking at something we could no longer see. We wondered if once we were a part of this, if this was where we had come from, if this had been our life. If once we had belonged here.

'What did we come here for?' I asked the child.

Suddenly I didn't know where we had come from let alone why we were here. Surely the mountain hut was long ago. A lifetime before this one. Our hut was rapidly fading from sight over the horizon of our minds.

'I'm lost,' she said.

I was lost too. Streets were heading off in all directions. Buildings and more buildings. Bridges and more bridges. Towers and glass windows. Alleyways and underpasses. And people. People going about their daily business. People going in and out of doorways. Pedestrians busy being pedestrians. Keeping their pedestrian faith. Everybody appearing to be alive. People talking on their cellphones. Whispering into invisible mics. Building things out of words as they strode along.

'We're lost because we're frightened,' I said.

'That must be it,' she said.

'We need to get out of here,' I said.

'I lost my coat,' she said. 'I don't know where it is. It gets cold at night.'

'Maybe you left it back at that other place,' I said.

'What other place?'

There was a place. Lots of rooms and people coming and going. Stairways everywhere. The little girl had been there, playing the piano like a child prodigy. Up and down the scale like water flowing forward and backward. Nobody there knew anything.

We wandered along, in and out of the shadows of buildings, past empty doorways and polished windows. Some dogs had started to follow us. I didn't like the look of them. They didn't like the look of us. They were sniffing the air, trying to catch our scents.

'Over there,' she said, 'there's a wharf. We could catch a ferry.'

A ferry would get us away from these omnipresent streets. They had no end. They curved everywhere. The wharf people were sitting in seats waiting. Their faces blank, like mudcake creatures. They were sitting in blank seats. Waiting. Beyond them was another wharf, with more people waiting. We started walking, passing wharf after wharf with people waiting and no ferry coming, and dogs following along behind.

The wharf people couldn't see us and stared past us with blank faces. I found it unnerving. They found the dogs unnerving.

'There's a ferry coming,' the girl said.

'I have no money,' I said. I was starting to panic. What had I done with my money? I might have left it at that other place, with lots of rooms, where the girl played the piano. It could have been stolen; the people there had too many hands. I started searching through my pockets. I needed to catch the ferry to find my body. I would find my body on the other side of the water. Without my body I was nothing.

I looked up. The little girl had gone. The dogs had gone. The seats where the wharf people had been waiting were empty. Blank and empty.

My pockets were empty.

The eyes of the ferryman were like the eyes of the little girl, huge and blank.

I was a blank.

I was nothing.

I was back in the hut. This seamless transition unnerved me. There was no sensation of coming back into my body like waking from a sleep. I had no body to come back into. I hadn't been sleeping because I was never awake. The ferry had never arrived. The ferryman hadn't collected his fee.

I was still frightened.

I had failed to find my real body and I didn't know if I had been incinerated, dropped to the bottom of the ocean or buried deep underground. Abandoned in a mass grave. I felt responsible for the body I no longer had, or had any use for.

I am running through a field. My feet have no weight. The sky has no weight. The world is borne forward while I am carried upwards. The air is charged with suppressed energy, the sky as tight as a coiled spring. The field is filled with yellow flowers and lush green grass. Dandelion, daisy, calendula, cowslip and cosmos. They release their scent into my hands, soft as moths. The field is a movement. One tawny movement. The field is uncoiling. I am uncoiling. The field never stops. It is like walking across the petals of one vast flower. I am carefree. I open with the yellow light. This is the happiest moment of my life because I am walking through the field of yellow flowers. A medley of yellow flowers. Under a satin sun. And springy grass. Light springs off the grass. I sing through my feet. Joy everywhere. Inside and out. I can partake of it, drink from the cup. Breathe it in. Breathe it out. Lift it up, lift it out. Hold it in, let it shout. Let your song run about. And excitement. If I jumped into the air, it would buoy me, hold me, lift me, cup me.

I can jump across valleys from hilltop to hilltop. In my hands, a skipping rope to skip wherever I want. Skip, flip, over the hills and far way. I can skip across rooftops; I can jump over the sky. I can fly. I can skim the gravity fields of planets. I can jump from creation to creation without turning a hair. I know joy because joy is there to be known. The joy is in the movement. The joy is the movement.

I sing, my voice as pure as feathers.

In that excitement I am on the edge of something stupendous, something beyond all the imaginings of mankind. Beyond our fondest gestures. A place where words can never go, for the stupendous cannot be described. Only the wordless can follow.

It is a place not to see but to behold.

At that very moment, at that apex, in the midst of that explosion of delight, I feel the first chill touch of the shadow, the shadow that grows out of stale corners. The shadow that makes a home for itself in my body. My toes go first, as if they've been amputated. My feet loose themselves. They hardly know where to go. The field is there but my feet are not. My feet are dead. They thump against the ground like lumps of wood. Numbness seeps upwards, passing a bow wave through my whole body. My body begins to tingle. Violet plasma leaps from the faces of the yellow flowers. I hammer my legs with my fists but feel nothing. They can walk but they can't feel. I am walking on stilts. My hips are growing numb. Ants are running up and down my arm, on the inside. I go blue dizzy, yellow blind. The yellow flowers turn into a blur. Streaks of colour across my eyeballs, dust in my blood.

I am dying by degrees. Piece by piece. If this is what the living consider an instant death, that instant is drawn out to eternity. I know when the numbness reaches my heart, it will stop and everything will stop, and I will fall among the yellow flowers. Fall hard among the yellow flowers. I am reassured by the fact that *they* are not dying. They are not allowed to die. They have to always be there, for all time, in the never-ending field.

With a dream you can wake up. You can find yourself somewhere else. With a memory you are trapped. Trapped by the events as they happen. Trapped by the things you did and didn't do.

If I was looking to know how I died, my run through the field of yellow flowers was as near as I was going to come. I am prepared for the field to be imaginary, I could have been lying in a hospital bed or in a ditch by the side of the road. I can't be sure about those yellow flowers even though I know their names, but the numbness was real. The drifting deadness made me what I am today. It crept everywhere. It stopped my heart. It stopped the guns. It stopped the whisper of blood. My mind blazed up in a luminous plasma, and I found myself on the track to the mountain hut, dressed in my funeral suit.

I can't believe that's all I'm going to get, that I'm never going to find out how I lived, whether I was a good person or a murderer, whether I died a natural or a violent death, whether I had lived honourably, stayed out of a life of crime, whether I smiled with my heart or my eyes, whether I helped the child on the road who was lost, who had nowhere to go, whose hand sought mine, whether I walked away or towards...

I remembered all this as I stood outside the hut with the child, watching the elements grow strange and wild.

'I thought I'd learned more than this,' I said.

'I want to go home,' the child said.

'Me too,' I said.

But home was just a word.

The air trembled. The colours of the world turned dark. A ball of violet plasma passed from one peak to another. I knew this was a natural electrical phenomenon, like an intense form of static, and might signal a coming storm. We went to the vantage point to see if it might come again. The child sat solemnly on the rock and looked around at the world so far below it was hard to tell if it was there or not. Purplish cloud arched over us. There was a bluish tinge to the air. The wind rose and fell like an ocean. The far-off land was shot through with streaks of light.

I wanted to tell the child that I would unravel all the mysteries. All the bits between. Like a jigsaw puzzle. Every last piece. Until I had completed the picture.

'I remember things,' I said, 'But I'm not sure the memories are mine.'

'Whose are they?'

'Who knows? Maybe memories just float about like patches of mist. Free floating memories. They could be anybody's.'

'That's funny.'

When the body dies memories might just float away, I thought. They have nothing to anchor them.

'Passing clouds,' I said.

She seemed to understand. 'Do you want to be solid again?'

'I don't think so,' I said. But thoughts were thin. They had no purchase. 'I feel things, but I'm not sure the feelings are mine.'

'Whose are they?'

'Who knows? Maybe feelings just float about like patches of mist. Free floating feelings. They could be anybody's.'

'That's funny.'

I agreed with her. Feelings with nothing to anchor them.

'I dream things,' I said, 'But I'm not sure the dreams are mine.'

'Whose are they?' This time she was smiling. Her teeth were dark purple.

'Who knows? Maybe dreams just float about like patches of mist. Free floating dreams. They could be anybody's.'

'That's funny.'

'Passing clouds.' Dreams with nothing to anchor them.

We laughed. The conversation had become fun. All these things, dreams feelings memories, floating around like colours on a boundless canvas. Circling. Repeating themselves. Nothing to anchor them.

'Look!' the child was pointing back to the hut. St Elmo's fire was dancing on the roof. It was green turning into yellow. On the tin roof that was turning puce.

We watched it for a while.

'We can't stay here forever,' the child said.

What's forever? I wondered.

I saw Ada Camara again. She was not a part of my mountain world. Ada belonged entirely to life. There was no hint of death about her. Her black skin shone like the mountain sky at night. Her breath was full of tropical heat. Her hair was like an ocean rising and falling in the wind. We were running. We were holding hands. We were running and holding hands. Her hand was strong and warm. Her grip was firm. We were not running towards anything or away from anything. We were neither hunter nor hunted. We ran for the joy of running. The sky was running too. Running with us. Everything else was moving backwards. Backwards was where the past lay. Ahead of us landscapes with deserts and cities were coming into view. Always coming into view.

Soon my legs grew tired. Ada was inexhaustible. I was the runt of the litter, always being left behind, always with tired legs, always playing catch up. Ada swung me up onto her shoulders. She was so strong and I was so light. Her orchard fragrance was laced with sweat. I wrapped my legs around her neck and held on to her thick black hair and off she ran, me swaying on top. Her legs were so mighty she could stride right over chasms and mountains.

We lay on a beach, under an indigo sky. Either way we looked, the beach stretched off to infinity. The jade sea barely moved. We were alone but for a single distant tree with yellow blossoms. We were naked. The heat was mellow. The heat was trickling down my chest. And hers. The heat was trickling between my legs. And hers. We were both trickling. Soon we came together, chest to chest, trickle to trickle, heat to heat. Our heat mingled. Her hand was buried in my ocean. I cried. The first sound a human being will make in the world. That moment of joyful outrage.

The lone tree with the yellow blossom echoed my cry. The sky caught it. The sky turned from indigo to beryl. The sea turned to silk. The blossoms fell softly to lie around the bottom of the tree, a circle of yellow flowers like a fallen skirt.

I was on my bunk in the hut, staring at the ceiling. Like the sky, it kept changing colour. A light rain was sweeping across the roof in gusts. The fire was out. One moment I was with Ada on a beach, the next moment I was staring at the cold grate.

The child was lying on the other bunk. I got up and walked around the hut, feeling the floor connect with my feet. Below the floor was rock. And below the rock there was more rock. As I approached the other bunk the little girl put her arms up over her face. 'I'm not going to hurt you,' I said. She lowered her arms but I could see her fear. This was so different from the night before, when we had shared a fire in companionship. There had been no fear then, merely curiosity. Fascination even.

'You killed me,' she said.

I stepped back in shock. I put my arms up over my face. A terrible blow was about to fall. I closed my eyes and saw a swimming darkness. Monstrous shapes surged beneath the surface. I trembled, pierced by the light of the farthest stars.

I opened my eyes. The child was holding on to her side in a curious gesture, as if she were staunching blood. She died wounded, died before her time.

Died in her own blood on the side of the road. Died in her own sad blood.

And I had killed her. With my own sad hands. I had been with Wilson Harris. Together we had been walking through a broken landscape shooting people at will, shooting men, women, children. The sky above us was as hard as stone.

I didn't say anything. I didn't have any words.

We remained like that for some time. Notional hours turned into notional days. Adult and child, murderer and murdered, we remained through the notional hours and the notional days.

After eons had passed, I said, 'I think you died in a war. I was a soldier. I kept that old army blanket. I kept it because it smelled of the past.'

'You killed me because you couldn't bear your love,' she said.

A sad wisdom. There was never a time when there was no war.

Our lonely occupation of the hut was interrupted by the arrival of two trampers. They appeared at the door, as if out of nowhere, dressed in army fatigues and carrying rifles. They didn't see us. We stood off to one side, out of their way. Briefly, I wondered what would happen if they walked right through us.

They threw their packs down and sat wearily at the table. With some laughing and heaving, they pulled off each other's boots, and removed their trousers which were muddy and wet. One was a solid woman with muscly legs and the other was a wiry man with hairy legs.

They looked right past us. We stood in the corner of the room and watched them as they sat side-by-side at the table, with their legs touching, comparing photos on their cellphones, cooing when they found a good one. We didn't know what they were looking at, but I had a feeling it wasn't mountain scenery. We could have got close enough to look over their shoulders, but refrained. A sense of delicacy held us back. We didn't want to haunt them; we weren't that kind of dead.

I was not envious of their messy, sweaty physicality, the creaks and groans of their bodies, the rumble of digestion, their squeaks and farts, not even when they got on one of the bunks and made love with that particular abandon people feel when they are many miles from anybody else.

We left the hut when that started, and went to hang out by our vantage point. There was nothing for us to do. The living have objectives. They want to shoot things, take photos and make love. They have things to do and places to go. People to meet and deals to make. People to love and people to hate. It's the human world. Everybody's on the brink of something. About to make a fortune or lose it. Find love or lose it. Find life or lose it. Stare destiny in the face. But we had nowhere to go and no one to meet. Our destiny was a thing of the past. We'd gone over the event horizon. All we had to keep us going were unanswered questions about our lives and our deaths.

This mountain top and hut was the last place on earth. Our last place on earth. The last outpost of human occupation. There was nothing above us but the sky. Everything else was behind us, the earth tipping into emptiness.

'Now we know,' the child said, gesturing towards the hut.

'What?'

'What we don't want.'

'What we don't want,' I repeated. That was true. The dead have no lust for life. No desire to take flesh once more. To walk around in pleasure or pain. To suffer and face death. Don't ask us to be reborn.

I had the feeling that the child knew something that I didn't. Her face was very composed, her manner calm. I waited for her to tell me, but she didn't. She held the knowledge inside herself. I wanted to sweep her up and hold her to my bosom as if she were my child. If I held her tight enough she would become a part of me, and I would know all that she knew.

I had an intimation then of how this was going to end. The shadow being in the doorway was larger than time.

We stayed there all night, watching the stars pass into and out of existence. We didn't feel the passing of time. Like the wind, time passed right through us. We might have spent an eternity there and hardly noticed it. Eternity was all around us, wheeling about like a great bird with starry wings.

In the morning, the two campers hung around. It seemed they were reluctant to leave. I think they wanted to make love again but neither of them were ready to act on it. They lingered over making breakfast, and afterwards sat in the doorway like a couple of lizards sunning themselves. They were waiting for it to happen.

Then I remembered my experience in the beech forest, how I had suffused my being into it, and how I felt that if I held the child hard enough we would merge the way I merged with the rain. We had a porous interface with the physical world. The interpenetration of matter and spirit.

Now was the time.

'I know what I have to do,' I said.

'You're going away,' the child said.

I began to move towards the campers. Slowly and carefully as if I might otherwise disturb them, as if I needed to creep up on them.

'Don't do that,' the child said from behind me. 'You can't do that.'

But I could. And I would.

I was in my adult hermaphrodite form. It is the form in which I feel the most complete, the most inclusive. It didn't matter which of the campers I chose for this most intimate of incursions, but I ended up choosing the man as he seemed the earthiest and most connected to the mountain and hut.

'You don't want to do that.' The child said. 'You know that you died. That's enough to know, isn't it? What more can you know?'

'I need the agency of a living soul,' I said.

'No, you don't.' The child ran around in front of me as if she could interpose herself between me and the trampers. She seemed smaller and younger. Not much more than a toddler.

'I feel like I haven't died properly,' I said. 'A part of me is hanging on because there is something to find out. Knowledge will lead to wisdom and wisdom will lead to love and that will be an end to it.'

I needed to live again, albeit briefly, in someone else's flesh.

The child stood aside, tears streaking her face.

I didn't do anything special. I just walked right up to the camper and into him. I became one with his living body.

Life crashed in on me like a storm. I was jolted into the flesh. All the sights sounds and tastes were at full volume. I could feel the chill air passing in and out of the man's lungs, feel the shifting around in his gut from digestion and the heat coming up from his desire for the woman. I could feel his heart slushing away, and the ringing of the blood through arteries and veins. When he moved, I could feel the creaking of his bones and the tension in his musculature. Gravity held everything in place. When he stood up the man had to lift the sky on his shoulders. The morning sunlight lit countless tiny fires on his skin.

This is what it felt like to be alive and have a body. Messy, painful and pleasurable all at once.

He picked up his cellphone and aimed it around. For a moment it settled on the child. The man peered at the screen. Through his eyes I saw the child. He lowered the camera and raised it again. The child was still there. The cellphone fell through his numb fingers and clunked down onto the stony ground. His breath was short and ragged, harsh in his chest.

He stepped backwards and nearly fell.

'What's the matter?' the woman said.

'Nothing.' He bent over to pick up his cellphone. Blood rushed into his head. Fear was constricting his heart. He looked around for his rifle.

Holding the cellphone steadied him. He laughed. A big hollow sound. Casually, he swung the cellphone around. There was no child. He tried to line up some interesting shots of the woman, wanting to catch her off guard.

As he did so, memories poured through his head. There was love and violence all mixed up. Something terrible happened to the man he didn't want to think about. Desiring the woman triggered it, blighting him with fear and uncertainty. I saw his past and his love affair with the camera. He used his cellphone to distance himself from the things around him by framing them, objectifying them, putting himself at one remove from them by photographing them.

His desire triggered his grief, which triggered mine. My emotions came flooding back on the wings of his. I didn't see images with the sharp clarity of the visions I'd had of Ada and the old man on the veranda, but I recognised that what I was apprehending were feelings from a life once lived. I saw a woman on her knees bent over a bath, trying to drown a three months old baby by holding it underwater. Her face was a mask of torment, like the face of a fiend. I was looking up at it through the water, struggling for air. I was the baby and this was my first death.

She couldn't go through with it and pulled me out, tipping me over to drain the water out. For the rest of my life, however, I could feel water in my lungs, not knowing what the feeling was. Now I knew that the moment in the bath with my mother holding me down was my true death. The life I had lived subsequently, its rise and fall, were but a shadow of this moment. The baby that grew up and had a life was not the baby who died in the bathtub. That baby was me. I had been dead right from the start.

I had my answer. The only answer I needed.

The man began to sob. The camera dangled from his hand. The sobs shook his ribcage. His tears felt like hot blood running down his cheeks. His body folded up. He was lying on the sharp ground. His hands clawed at the rock.

The woman came over and put her arms around him and held him. He surrendered himself to her.

I had no reason to stay. I didn't belong in this man's body. I didn't need to live through the tumult of what was about to happen between him and the woman. I floated out of his flesh and reformed my imaginal body.

The campers made love outside in the sunshine and then decamped. As they packed, their chatter was all about how they were going to get off the mountain. They knew all about the washed-out path, and were discussing other possible routes, as well as the weather. They were nervous, and there was something they didn't want to talk about.

Before they left, they took some photos of the hut. I stood at the hut door and smiled for the camera. A few hours after they left, I heard a helicopter somewhere far off. It drifted in and out of hearing.

Alone. And not alone. The universe, in its roar and sparkle, surrounds me.

The dawn of creation is at my fingertips. It begins and ends here.

The sky keeps changing colour as if it has lost its memory of itself.

This inky sky on which the will of night is written.

The great, overflowing bowl of the sky at dawn.

The mountain slopes away into nothingness.

It is a construction of light.

It is beginning to dissolve, to fall in upon itself. That might take a million years, but a million years can happen in an instant.

There is only me to hold it in place, and I am nothing more than the flickering tail end of the body's St Elmo's fire. I hide inside the doorways of myself, but only as long as the moment that holds me.

Soon the mountain will become an aurora. Then it will be erased.

The distant plain has gone. There is only void and sunlight.

Beyond that there is no sunlight. And there is no dark.

The absence of light is not dark but velvet.

The absence of dark is not light but silk.

I join myself in the present tense. My future is already in the past. The past becomes present. It's all rolled up into a single scroll.

It becomes running water, a mountain stream.

I was. I am. I am not. I will, but not be.

From the tenses I created a see-saw, back and forth, to spin some sense of time and causality, a movement from then to there, from there to now, and back again. From that see-saw a narrative is born, an imaginal body brought into being.

I can't stay forever on the fulcrum of the see-saw, one foot forward, one back, poised between the no longer and the not yet.

With nothing to anchor the past, the future has no cogency.

The visitor's book is empty. There are no scrawled entries. No expressions of wonder.

Whatever it is I have learned must now be forgotten. It holds me to the past, to words, and all they can contain.

And the words too, all written on air, turn liminal, and are gone.

End

Mike Johnson, fiction writer and poet, is widely regarded as one of New Zealand's most innovative writers. He lives on Waiheke Island and has taught creative writing at AUT University and the University of Auckland. In 2002 he received The University of Auckland's Literary Fellowship, having been Literary Fellow at Canterbury University in 1987. His first novel, *Lear, the Shakespeare Company Plays Lear at Babylon* was short listed for the New Zealand Book Awards in 1986, his novel *Dumb Show* won the Buckland Memorial Award for Literary Excellence in 1995, and he won the Frances Kean Award his short story, 'Magic Strings' in 1999. His first book of poetry, *The Palanquin Ropes*, (1983) was co-winner of the John Cowie Reed Memorial Competition. His non-fiction, *Angel of Compassion*, was shortlisted for the Ashton Whyle Award in 2014, and a poem from *Vertical Harp, The selected poems of Li He* (2006) has been anthologised in the *Essential New Zealand Poems: Facing the Empty Page* (Random House, 2015). Mike Johnson is the author of twenty-six books including nine books of poetry, three of shorter fiction, one non fiction, three children's books, and ten novels.

Also by Mike Johnson

Novels
Stench
Driftdead
Lethal Dose
Zombie in a Spacesuit
Hold My Teeth While I Teach You to Dance
Travesty
Counterpart
Dumbshow
Antibody Positive
Lear: The Shakespeare Company Plays Lear at Babylon

Shorter Fiction
Confessions of a Cockroach/Headstone
Back in the Day: Tales of NZ's Own Paradise Island
Foreigners

Poetry
Selected Poems
Sketches
The Raising Light Trilogy
Ladder With No Rungs, Illustrated by Leila Lees
Two Lines and a Garden, Illustrated by Leila Lees
To Beatrice: Where We Crossed the Line
Vertical Harp: The Selected Poems of Li He
Treasure Hunt
Standing Wave
From a Woman in Mt Eden Prison & Drawing Lessons
The Palanquin Ropes

Non-Fiction
Angel of Compassion

Children's Books
Flippity Fluppity Flop, Illustrated by Daniela Gast
A House With No Windows, Illustrated by Ingrid Berzins
Kenni and the Roof Slide, Illustrated by Jennifer Rackham
Taniwha. Illustrated by Jennifer Rackham